EMILY the Giraffe

Pascal Lemaître

Hyperion Books for Children
New York

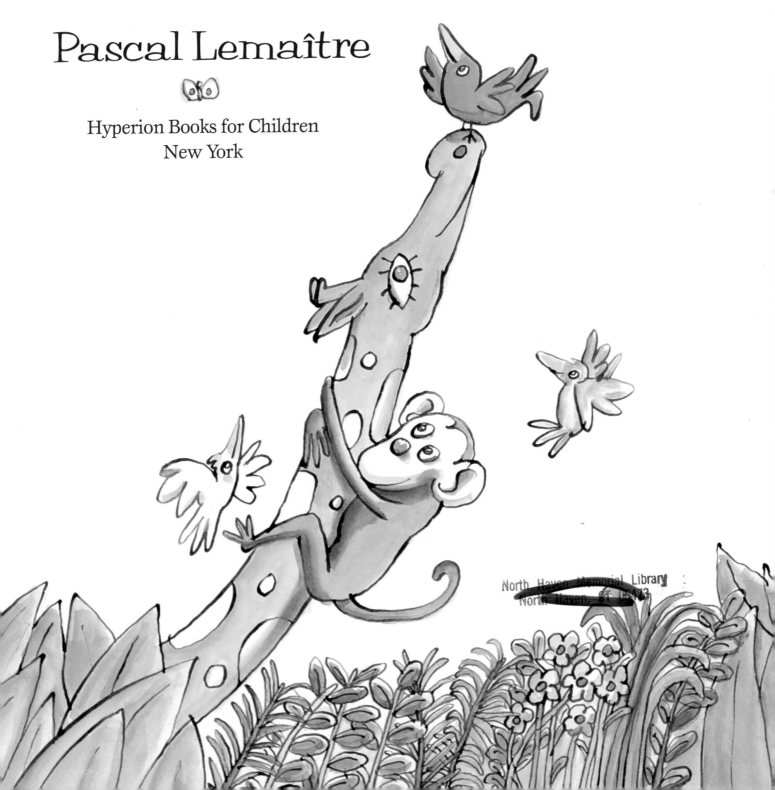

Emily the Giraffe loved to frisk about in the hot African sun. The whole of the bush was her playground.

Emily's favorite game was turning somersaults. Another of her special tricks was twisting her body into the number 9. All the animals adored Emily. She was such a great sport.

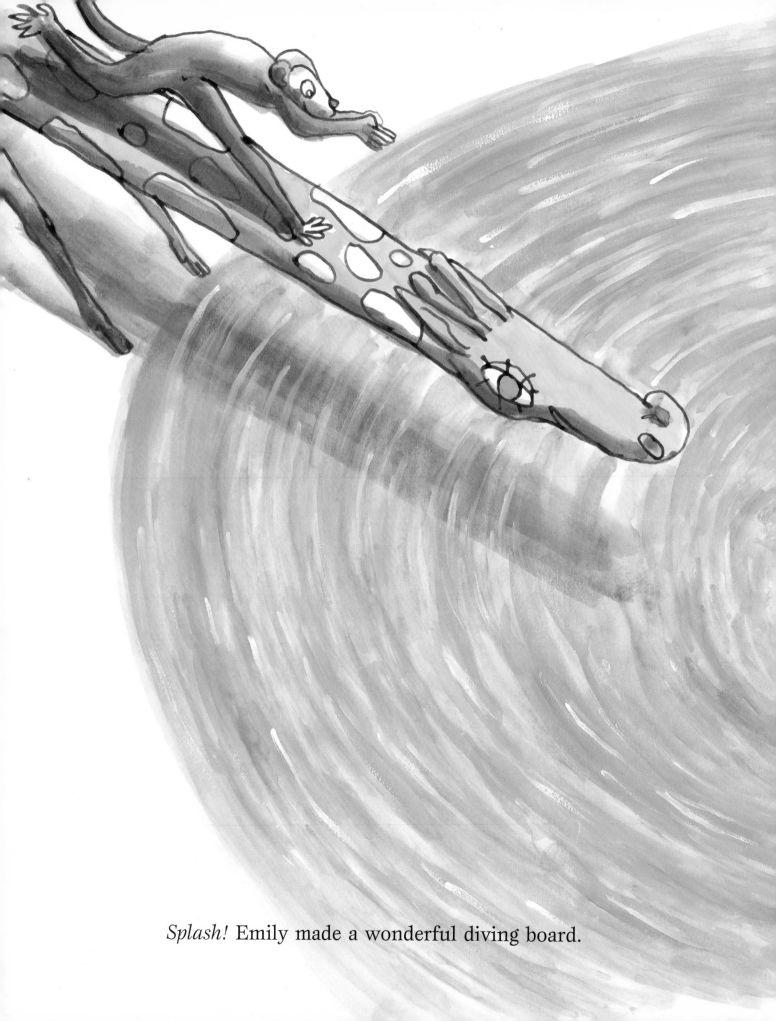

Splash! Emily made a wonderful diving board.

And the markings on her back came in very handy
for playing chess! Emily and her friends could play
anywhere, at any time.

Her friends could always count on Emily. When Bird's tree blew down, Emily moved the whole family, complete with nest, in one trip.

Each morning Emily would call on her neighbors. She chatted with friends at the top of the highest tree and the bottom of the deepest hole.

Everyone wanted to be just like Emily. The little snails
were very proud of having horns just like hers.

Then one day something dreadful happened. A shortsighted butterfly collector accidentally caught Emily in his enormous net. He was very embarrassed and apologized wholeheartedly.

To make amends, he invited Emily to return with him to his homeland in the north for a visit. As she had never been abroad, Emily readily accepted his kind offer.

Her friends were sad to see her go and gathered to bid her bon voyage. Emily and the butterfly collector sailed on a steamship for days and days....

When they arrived, Emily found all the hustle and
bustle very exciting. She quickly made new friends and
was always eager to lend a hand—or neck—when needed!

One morning she met a chimney sweep with a ladder as tall as she was! He offered her a position as his assistant. The two of them spent many days cleaning chimneys.

But the job had its drawbacks. Emily's neck stretched and stretched, and the soot got into her lungs. The doctor prescribed rest, fresh air, plenty of vitamins, and bathing in the sea. So off Emily went to the seashore. She soon felt so much better that when the circus came to town she decided to join.

Emily loved showing off her tricks under the big top.
On her days off, Emily went sailing with her friend the
clown. But soon the circus moved on. Emily didn't want
to leave the seaside, so she stayed behind.

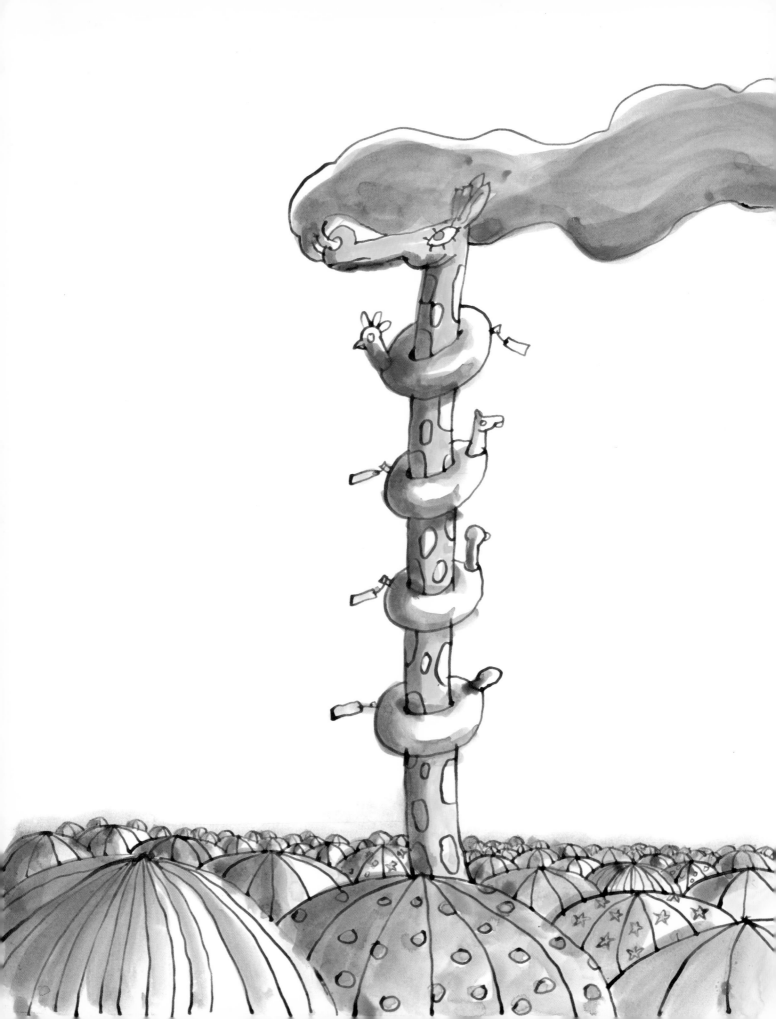

Her new job was selling rubber rings on the beach. One day thick black smoke filled the sky. It floated above the beach umbrellas and tickled Emily's nose. Fire! Before the fire engine had even arrived, Emily saved a little girl and her teddy bear from the flames.

The king gave Emily a wonderful medal for bravery. The queen offered to grant Emily her dearest wish.

What ever would she wish for? A trip to the North Pole? A rocket ride to the moon? Emily didn't need but a moment. She knew exactly what she wanted.

And that is how Emily returned to the African bush.
All her friends cheered to have her home again!

Text and illustrations © 1993 by Rainbow Grafics Intl–Baronian Books, S. C.
All rights reserved.
Printed in Belgium.
First published 1991 by Rainbow Grafics Intl–Baronian Books,
32 rue de la Vallée, 1050 Brussels, Belgium.
First published in the United States of America by Hyperion Books for Children,
114 Fifth Avenue, New York, New York 10011.

First Edition
1 3 5 7 9 10 8 6 4 2

Library of Congress Catalog Card Number: 92-85508
ISBN: 1-56282-403-1 / 1-56282-404-X (lib. bdg.)

The type for this book is set in 16-point ITC Esprit Book.